OUT OF

A MARLIN CHRONICLES NOVELLA

Alyson Mountjoy

ISBN: 9781521122327

DEDICATION

This novella is all about friendship, so I am dedicating it to my few true friends. Children often have many friends, but as we get older the numbers diminish as we find the ones that stay the course through bad times as well as good. To my mind, a true friend is not someone who always agrees with you, or someone with whom you have everything in common. A true friend is a person who is always there for you no matter what, standing in your corner against the world, and they know that you will always do the same in return without question. They laugh with you and they cry with you, and they're not afraid to tell when you're wrong. They encourage you and believe in your dreams as if they were their own. They know when you need help before you know it yourself, and they often give it without being asked.

True friendship is unchanging, without constraint, or conditions. It isn't just about the good times. You can pick it up after ten, twenty years or more, and it will still feel the same and mean the same. It is loyalty and trust; it is giving without expecting anything in return. True friendship is rare; it is a meeting of souls, and it is a blessing; a gift.

I'm lucky, because I have some true friends. My husband and children are also my friends, and these qualities thrive in them too. So, if you are blessed with a true friend, cherish them as they cherish you. Show them, tell them and never take that gift for granted. Your life will never be the same without them.

"I would rather walk with a friend in the dark, than alone in the light."

Helen Keller

OUT OF MARLIN

IT WAS ABOUT eleven o'clock on the morning of Saturday, 5th February 2016, and Stephanie Meares and Jan Matthews had been driving for almost three hours. Stephanie had reluctantly agreed to a trip with Jan, her blonde, gorgeous, oldest and dearest friend. After the stresses and strains of the past few months, she had to admit that they both needed a break, and she had reluctantly succumbed to Jan's pleas to put herself first for a change.

Since arriving in the village of Marlin in June the previous year, life had been tumultuous in the extreme. Stephanie had finally learned to accept and develop her psychic ability, something which the villagers referred to as "the gift," which had laid dormant for many years. Jan was already well-attuned to hers since early childhood. Stephanie had repeatedly used that gift in recent months, helping those around her, but it had taken its toll, and she was exhausted. So, Jan had dragged her from her responsibilities (and her seaside cottage) to spend a weekend away.

Marlin was a pretty village on the Cornish coast; it was a magical place, and Stephanie was homesick already. Rarely had she left Marlin for any length of time since moving there the previous year, with the intention of writing her second novel. To her surprise, Marlin was more to her now than just an escape to solitude from the hustle and bustle of London; it had turned out to be the only place that she had ever felt truly happy since leaving her childhood home at 18. In Marlin, she had found a place where she could finally put down roots.

Jan still lived in London and she had stayed overnight with Stephanie at her cottage, The Lodge, so that they could make an early start on their journey the next day. Unfortunately, a couple of bottles of wine and a late night had led to their departure being somewhat delayed.

Having left Maisy her cat in the capable care of a reputable cat-sitter from the village, Stephanie felt a pang of guilt. Truth be told she hated leaving her, and Maisy deeply resented being left. She would no doubt make her pay for the perceived abandonment with pouting and other forms of disdain on her return, and for some time afterwards.

"You spoil that cat, Steph," Jan was saying. "You

know I love her as much as you do, but you have to have a life too!"

"You don't understand because you don't have a pet," Stephanie replied in a measured tone as she drove. "It's a responsibility I take very seriously, as you well know."

It was a discussion which they had revisited now and again over the years. It normally ended with them agreeing to disagree, which is what happened now.

Jan was a private investigator and her company also provided a service in ridding clients of unwanted spirit visitors. They had both agreed that the trip was to be a work-free zone, and there was to be no mention of anything involving business, writing, spirits, Marlin, London, disastrous past relationships, or other matters that might seek to ruin the restful aims of their weekend break. They had even agreed to turn off their phones for the duration, which she thought Jan would find difficult because it was usually not far from her hand or her ear. But so far, she had stuck to the agreement without a whimper or a relapse. If anyone wanted them, they could wait till Monday. Far from being a difficult task,

Stephanie soon found that unplugging from the world and leaving all her baggage behind her was actually quite liberating, and slowly they relaxed into a holiday mood.

"At the next roundabout take the second exit!" demanded the satnav.

"Shut up Clarice!" said Stephanie. "You already got us lost twice in the last half hour!"

"Turn the stupid thing off," said Jan. "It's giving me a headache!"

"Well, if you hadn't had so much to drink last night…" said Stephanie smiling.

"Fair point. Can we stop for coffee again, please?" whined Jan, rubbing her temples.

"We only stopped an hour ago, and we're almost there. Can't you hang on half an hour?" Stephanie replied.

"If I have to!" said Jan feebly, swigging the last remaining mouthful from her bottle of elderflower flavoured water and enjoying the view from the window.

They were in South Wales, en route to a rented

cottage amidst wild mountains and vibrant valleys. Stephanie had chosen their destination, having enjoyed many holidays in Wales as a child. But she had never been to this part of Wales before, and Jan had never visited Wales at all, so they were both quite excited to see what it had to offer.

In fact, Stephanie loved everything about Wales: the warm, friendly people, the lilting language and strong persisting tradition of music, literature and poetry. It was also a country filled with legend and rich in folklore. She had already amassed a certain amount of vocabulary, a fact of which she was quite proud, and she had also read a lot of their folk tales. The Welsh scenery was breath-taking, little wonder that so many Welsh people were prone to sing in praise of its beauty, and were often loathe to leave it.

Welsh beaches were some of the best in the world, very similar to those of Cornwall with rocky vistas and rock pools, golden sand and towering cliffs. But today they were venturing inland. They were in search of a little solitude in a quiet village location surrounded by beautiful, open countryside. As they soon discovered, even in the bleak tail end of winter, the village of

Pentre Brân did not disappoint.

It was nestled near the bottom of a deep valley surrounded by tall, craggy mountains and grassy hills which undulated like a snake across the horizon. Along the valley floor ran a wide, fast-flowing river. Instead of feeling hemmed in as she expected to when she envisioned being surrounded by mountains, Jan was surprised at the illusion of space, probably due to width of the valley and the absence of many houses and people; they had only passed a smattering of farms along the way. After being raised in Bristol like Stephanie, and living for several years in London, she was used to either cityscapes, sprawling urban estates or the cosiness of compact seaside villages like Marlin. This was a new experience, and she loved it already.

The mountains, sprinkled with what she suspected were sheep, reached up to touch the sky. Their heads were literally in the clouds; it was a landscape befitting a scene from The Lord of the Rings, minus the Hobbits. Her eyes lit up when she saw the village, but her excitement was momentarily dampened by the way that the sky quickly darkened and heavy clouds blew in, blocking out the sun.

"Well, this is a bit ominous!" proclaimed Jan, looking disappointed as she lowered her immaculately shaped eyebrows into a frown.

Stephanie knew what she meant. The weather did change suddenly in the valleys, but this was something else. As they entered the village, all her senses became more alert; tingling with anticipation. On first inspection, the village appeared deserted and still. They were both surprised to find how similar it looked to Marlin, with its stone buildings and wealth of charm. But like Marlin, this was no ordinary village. They looked at each other without words. Already, they could feel it.

***

They soon found the cottage which Stephanie had rented. It was not difficult: the small, detached, stone cottage was the first that they came to as they entered Pentre Brân. It was on the right-hand side of the main road, with quite a gap between it and its nearest neighbour. To the left were open views across the valley.

Tŷ Nant (meaning "house of the stream") certainly lived up to its name. It was perched on the edge of a shallow brook which burbled its way along in search of a river, tumbling along in a melodic fashion over ancient pebbles like the tinkling of fairy bells. The water was as clear as molten diamonds.

Stephanie parked by the kerb. She had to smile as she stepped out of the car and took in her surroundings, along with a lungful of crisp, cool, Welsh air. As expected, the temperature was colder that Marlin by a good few degrees. But what made her shiver was the feeling which came over her as soon as she approached the cottage. She looked over at Jan who was closing the passenger door and raised her eyebrows. Jan nodded in agreement; she had felt it too. Tŷ Nant was unmistakeably haunted.

***

The cottage stood right there on the pavement with no driveway or front garden. Stephanie raised her hand to try the latch of the oak door which had heavy black hinges and was studded with black nails. It opened with a squeak.

"*Dewch i mewn,* come on in!" called a sing-song voice with a bilingual greeting.

"*Must be the owner,*" thought Stephanie.

Stephanie went in first with Jan close behind. There in the hallway at the bottom of the stairs stood a woman with wispy, grey hair fashioned in a bun. The hair clips poking out at various angles gave her a quizzical, dated appearance. She was wearing an old-fashioned, floral crossover apron over a thin, white, long-sleeved jumper and a skirt that was hidden beneath her apron, flat, and lace-up shoes.

"*Croeso,* welcome!" she said with a beaming smile. "I'm Mrs Jenkins. My niece Sarah is the one who sees to the lettings of the cottage. She will be here soon."

The woman's first language was obviously not English, but she was trying her best to make them feel welcome. She pointed to a comfortable cottage style sofa with a rose patterned cover and motioned for them to take a seat. Stephanie looked at Jan whose face was a picture of confusion. They sat down next to each other.

"Thank you, Mrs Jenkins," said Stephanie with a smile.

"Er, not the best weather today," offered Jan by way of conversation as the heavens opened and the window was lashed with heavy rain mixed with quite sizeable chunks of ice in the form of large hailstones.

"Oh, you'll be getting used to that round here!" said Mrs Jenkins smiling. "Changeable as anything!"

Jan smiled and made conversation while Stephanie looked around the room. The front door had opened straight into the cosy but small living room with thick, bare stone walls. The curtain fabric matched the chintz-covered sofa and chairs in shades of pink and green, and there was a green rug which was the type that had been handmade from rags. The deep window-sill and a small, oak dresser opposite contained a variety of floral patterned china and jugs, adding to the country-style ambience. It was as if they had stepped back in time.

An unlit open fire lay ready, directly opposite the door, and Stephanie could see straight through the opening in the chimney breast into another room beyond. She could just make out the legs of an oak dining table and several chairs. The room was spotlessly clean, and a collection of horse brasses near the fireplace gleamed eerily in the dismal light.

Opposite the sofa was a window with a view to a little patio and walled garden. The window was the only one in the room and it was also small, so the room was quite dark. At the end of the hall past the stairs she had noticed what looked like the kitchen.

Then the latch of the front door clicked, making them jump. Stephanie and Jan turned to see a woman of about forty. She rushed inside, shaking the shower from her umbrella and resting it in the base of a dark, oak coat stand that stood there. She seemed surprised to see them.

"Oh, hello," she said, "you must be my guests for the weekend!" Her English was far better, but her words still carried a rich, Welsh accent.

"Yes," said Jan, "your… aunt let us in." Jan said.

She turned back and the older woman had vanished

"I'm so sorry, I wish she wouldn't keep doing that!" said the woman in a matter-of-fact way. "I'm Sarah Jenkins, by the way."

Stephanie and Jan introduced themselves.

"She doesn't know then, that she's…" said Jan.

"Dead? No, not a clue!" said Sarah with a grin. "Aunty Bessie passed over in 1992, and she's been welcoming guests ever since! Most of them don't even see her, and others run off when they realise. But you're different, aren't you?" she added, with a wistful stare.

"Yes, we're used to it!" said Stephanie. "She was very kind," she added.

"Would you like us to, sort of, you know…" Jan began, tentatively.

"Move her on, you mean? Oh, no, I wouldn't dream of it. This was her house you see, she left it to me. She won't bother you again. Once I turn up, she gets the hint and leaves till the next guests arrive! She belongs here, but she's not doing my business much good!" said Sarah with a nervous laugh.

"Understood," said Stephanie with a warm smile. Jan nodded.

"OK, then, here are your keys," Sarah said, dropping them into a china dish on a small table by the door. "There's fresh milk, butter and cheese in the fridge, a loaf of bread in the bread bin and you'll find tea and coffee on the shelf above the kettle. The beds are all aired and ready, and the electricity is included in the rental price. I'll pop in and see you before you leave on Monday morning. If you need anything, my number is on the card on the dresser. Have a lovely weekend, and, er, thanks for being so understanding!"

Without waiting for a reply, Sarah shot them a pleasant smile and hurried back out into the rain. Stephanie looked at Jan and they both burst out laughing.

"Well that was interesting! Now, where's the coffee?" said Jan, heading for the kitchen. To her disappointment, it turned out to be instant coffee, but it would have to do.

"Tea for me, please!" said Stephanie. "I'll collect our bags from the car," she added, peering out through the small window and seeing that the rain had eased considerably.

Ten minutes later their bags were at the foot of the stairs and they were sitting in the dining room. Lunch consisted of the fresh bread and delicious local cheese, followed by some fruit that they brought with them.

"After we unpack, shall we take a look around the village? suggested Stephanie.

"Good idea," said Jan. "Although I doubt it will take long!"

"Yes, it's more like a hamlet. I get the impression that this weekend is going to be a bit of a busman's holiday," said Stephanie. "There seem to be spirits wherever we go!"

"I know what you mean, Steph," Jan replied rolling her eyes. "It's to be expected, I suppose. They're drawn to us."

"At least Mrs Jenkins has made herself scarce," said Stephanie.

"Yes," said Jan. "She was harmless enough." Then after finishing the last of her coffee, she added. "It's the other one that worries me!"

***

After washing their lunch dishes and leaving them to drain, Stephanie joined Jan in the only bedroom in the property. Twin-bedded, it was decorated similarly to the living room with a floral, cottage-style theme, but the print here was of smaller flowers in accents of yellow. A similar green, rag rug lay on the floor between the beds, which had their white wood headboards to the wall on the left of the room. The thick, stone walls here were whitewashed, and the ceiling sloped from above the beds down to a lower wall where a white, rustic-looking wardrobe stood. The only other furniture in the room was a pair of matching bedside cabinets with two drawers in each. The room had a timeless feel, and the bare floorboards creaked. This was a very old cottage.

Jan had picked the bed nearest the door and was unpacking a few clothes and other items. Stephanie placed her case on the wide windowsill by the bed and did the same. They unpacked without speaking as if afraid to disturb the heavy silence that hung over the room. It felt like the subdued atmosphere of a library, or even church, where people naturally stopped speaking or used hushed voices.

Stephanie went into the small bathroom which they had passed on the landing to put some toiletries on the shelves provided. She was pleased to see that although it was small, the owner had fitted in a shower cubicle, and an enamel roll-top bath which stood proudly on its own little clawed feet. Several leaf-green plush towels lay on a nearby stand, and a soap dish with tiny guest soaps sat on the windowsill by the sink along with two glasses, a bottle of hand wash and a small unopened pot of herbal hand cream with a local label.

"BE CAREFUL!" said a voice next to her ear, breaking the silence.

Stephanie jumped. She recognised the voice as that of her spirit guide, Lucas who she had recently become able to communicate with after fully accepting her gift. He had been with her all her life, as spirit guides always are, but only recently had she been able to see him. He stood beside her now, protective and ever vigilant, and a man of few words. As swiftly as he had arrived, so he was gone.

With her senses in high alert, Stephanie turned quickly to return to the bedroom, and as she did so she caught a glimpse of someone who was walking briskly past the doorway.

She stepped out onto the landing to see the back of a tall man. He was broad and looked heavy, yet his feet made no sound on the uneven floorboards. Her ears were ringing, a sign that meant to her that something paranormal was taking place.

"Jan!" she yelled anxiously.

"It's OK, I see him!" said Jan.

Stephanie ran back into the bedroom to see Jan backed into the corner of the room by the window, overshadowed by a massive spirit. He had dark brown hair and wore a check shirt and overalls with stout walking boots. When he turned to look at her momentarily, she saw that he seemed to be in his late forties. His attention focused once more on Jan who was chanting one of the few spells that she knew, and it seemed to be keeping him at bay. He was glaring at Jan and yelling at her.

"LEAVE!" he said.

Stephanie shouted to distract him. He turned quickly and lumbered towards her, covering the short distance between the window and door in the blink of an eye. He was almost toe to toe with her when she looked unwaveringly into his eyes.

"STOP!" she commanded.

To her surprise, he did.

"I'm sorry!" he said, looking like at Stephanie with the air of a small child who had been caught doing something that he shouldn't. Then he vanished, muttering something unintelligible which she decided was probably in Welsh.

"Well, that was unexpected," said Jan, sitting down on the edge of her bed, and running a hand through her blond hair. Stephanie sat down next to her.

"Yes. He didn't want to be here," Stephanie answered. "I could sense it. Someone made him come here to put the fear of God into us. When he realised it wasn't going to work, he left."

"But why? Who the hell would want to scare us away?" asked Jan.

"I have no idea, but Lucas warned me about him so it must be serious. Anyway, we won't find out sitting here!" Stephanie said. "Let's take a walk around the village."

***

It was mid-afternoon by the time they had finished unpacking and set off to tour the village. The dark clouds had blown away down the valley, leaving a bright, but cold, winter afternoon in its wake. A rainbow spanned the river and several crows cawed enthusiastically from the bare treetops. It was as if they were sending a warning cry to herald the two strangers' presence.

"A murder of crows. Lovely!" said Jan.

"The village is named after them. *Pentre* comes from the Welsh word *pentref,* which means village, and *brân* means crows," Stephanie explained as they walked along.

"Appropriate," said Jan.

They soon covered the distance between their lodgings and a terrace of cottages which lined the street to their right. They continued along the main road of the village, and soon they came to another terrace perched on the side of the mountain to the left. The street began to feel enclosed and claustrophobic and a lot of the natural light had gone. It was as if the area was weighted with funereal reverence.

As they walked, they saw no-one, and all the blinds and curtains of the houses that they passed were drawn. It was as if the villagers were paying their respects to the dead, following the time-honoured tradition that when a hearse drove past, all curtains were drawn. Jan saw what might have been the twitch of a curtain, but that was all. In reality, it seemed like everyone was hiding.

"You'd think they would be used to tourists," Jan said.

"Yes, you would," said Stephanie pointedly.

On the right was a tea-room with an adjoining gift shop, then a shop selling walking and camping equipment. They were all empty apart from the staff who stood around with a resigned expression. It was off-season after all, so Stephanie thought no more of it: it was only natural that trade would be slow.

To the left of the tea-shop they saw a small supermarket with a surprisingly extensive range of fresh farm produce displayed outside. Then they found a traditional sweet shop with home-made fudge and toffee. They crossed over to inspect it. Jan, with her sweet tooth, was inside in a flash. Naturally, she had to try some samples, and she ended up buying a large selection which she stored safely in her large, purple, leather handbag. At the end of the row was a shop selling ladies' clothing for the wealthier, more mature customer. That shop was closed. They had still not seen a soul (living or otherwise) apart from the shop-keepers, and they all seemed remarkably wary of the new visitors.

At the end of the row of shops they came to a few more terraced houses. The three to the left probably had gorgeous views over the river from the back, and the four on the right backed onto the mountain. All had closed curtains and blinds. Then they reached a crossroads. A lane leading upwards on the left led to another small row of cottages and what looked like a dead end, and a road veering sharp right led to a row of newer, semi-detached properties that began slightly uphill and ran parallel with the shops. They walked a little way to the right; that route seemed to end somewhere behind Tŷ Nant, presumably on the other side of the garden wall. Beyond that was just the open countryside which they had passed on the way into the village. However, looming over the crossroads just a little further on, was a large pub with a striking sign. Jan's eyes lit up.

"We are on holiday…" she muttered beseechingly, at the sight of Stephanie's disapproving expression.

Stephanie sighed. "OK, but just one," she insisted.

Stephanie doubted that the pub would stock Jan's favourite dry, white wine or even a decent fruity red, but she followed her to the door. On reflection, she decided that a chilled orange juice would be most welcome.

The pub was named Y Ddraig Ddu, as depicted magnificently on the sign above the door, and Stephanie informed Jan that it meant The Black Dragon. A hand-written notice on the door itself revealed (in English and Welsh) that it provided excellent home-cooked meals. Unfortunately, another notice in the window informed the pair that it was only open in the day during the summer months.

"Never mind, we can come back later," said Stephanie, seeing Jan's deflated expression.

"Yes! At least that's dinner sorted!" said Jan with glee.

Stephanie knew full well that Jan wouldn't have been cooking anyway, due to a level of culinary ineptitude that she had rarely encountered in anyone. She was relieved to have the opportunity of a break from cooking. Although a capable cook herself, it was always a treat to have a meal prepared by someone else.

Stephanie had a funny feeling in the pit of her stomach as she looked at the ancient stone pub. It was on three floors and a glimpse through the nearest window showed her that it too had closed its curtains against prying eyes. She gazed upwards, and as she did so she spotted a face at an upstairs window at the top of the building. It was the face of a small, blonde girl. Her clothes were Victorian in style and her big, round eyes were the saddest that Stephanie had ever seen.

"Look!" she said and pointed up at her.

Jan looked up. "I can't see anything," she said. "But I can feel it. Terrible sadness."

Stephanie nodded and explained what she saw. "I haven't quite worked it out yet," she said "but something is very wrong with this village."

"I get the same feeling," said Jan. "Come on, let's go a bit further on and see what else we can find," she added cheerfully.

***

The road that led straight on from the village was covered in fog; the air was oppressive and threatening. They avoided that route. Stephanie remembered from looking at the map on her satnav that the main road continued to the next village, some distance away, and they had already discovered that the lane to the left led to a dead end. Midway between the main road and the route to the right that ran back behind Tŷ Nant they saw what looked like a bridle path, so they decided to follow it.

Stephanie knew that the stream that trickled next to their cottage had to have originated somewhere further up the mountain. So, they decided to try to trace it. As they left the confines of the village, they felt instantly lighter. It was as if a crushing blanket of negativity had been lifted.

The path to the right curved gently left after a while, taking them behind the mountain, and soon they couldn't see the village at all. They came to a plain bench, no more than a few planks of wood, but it was most welcome after the climb. The stream trickled past them on its well-worn route to the village.

Stephanie dipped her hand into the icy water and soon took it out again. It was so cold that it hurt her fingers. The sight of the fresh, clear water made them both thirsty. As tempting as the water looked, they knew that it wasn't clean enough to drink. They had both brought a bottle of water, and as they sat drinking, they shared some of the delicious, creamy fudge that Jan had bought. When they had caught their breath, Jan spoke first.

"It's so beautiful here, Steph!" she said.

"I know," Stephanie said. "Such a contrast to the village. It's like the whole place is overshadowed by something. Whatever it is, it's dark and nasty, and it doesn't want us here." Jan nodded.

"I think I know why," Stephanie continued. "The people in the village seem nervous and scared. Even that spirit we met in the bedroom. Whatever this is, they're scared of it, and they seem scared for us. But I think we can help them. And whatever is causing it knows it too," she said.

"Let's just relax and enjoy the peace and quiet for a bit," Jan said. "We can worry about that later."

The view over the next valley was worth the climb: it was spectacular. They could hear nothing except the constant chatter of the resident crows and the whisper of the stream. The sky was clear now, pale blue in the softening sunlight, with fingers of orange spreading out to herald the night. They had about an hour of light left, and the lack of cloud also meant that it was growing colder.

"Come on," Jan urged, jumping up, "let's go! It's cold sitting here, and I think we have a little more time left to explore before we need to start back."

"OK, but we'd better hurry," said Stephanie. "We don't want to be trapped up here in the dark!"

Her expression said it all; Pentre Brân was creepy enough in daylight.

***

They continued their journey along the path that curved around the mountain. A little farther on they came to a flat, grassy area. This place felt different; the air was heavy and still. There was no sound, like it had an impenetrable barrier around it. It was concealed from the view of the village and probably only known to people who took the time to climb up there. The friends shared a knowing glance; they had both sensed an atmosphere, an energy in the air as they stepped closer to what stood there.

In the centre of the clearing, surrounded by a circle of small rocks, was a tree. This was no ordinary tree. In the middle of winter high on a bleak Welsh mountain, this tree was covered with leaves. It was also covered in ribbons and bows, rags and pieces of string. At the base of the trunk was a selection of flowers and small toys.

"What the hell…?" said Jan.

"It's a wishing tree!" said Stephanie. "People tie ribbons and other items to it, and make a wish, or say a prayer for a lost loved one. I've read about them, but I've never seen one. I think it's a Pagan tradition. Many cultures use them to make offerings to various deities. Sometimes people would hammer a coin into a wishing tree in exchange for relief from an illness. Like an offering. But this one feels like a memorial of some sort."

"Wow!" said Jan. "What a beautiful sentiment."

"I know," Stephanie replied. "It doesn't explain why it has leaves in winter though, or the energy we can feel," she added. "It's really odd."

The circle was filled with a mix of emotions: love and joy, sadness and loss. It was a place of remembrance and mourning. But there was something else, something indiscernible prickling at the back of Stephanie's mind. Like a long-buried secret that she dared not release or remember. It felt surreal.

A breeze flew past them and they both started to shiver. Then clouds started to gather over the mountain above their heads.

"We'd better go," said Jan. "It's starting to get darker."

Stephanie didn't need to be asked twice; she turned and led the way back down to the village.

"We're not welcome here," she said as they walked.

Someone, or something, wanted them out of the village.

***

"That was quite a climb!" said Jan, as they sat in the kitchen as night drew in, with a hot drink and a chocolate biscuit or two.

"Well it was hardly Snowdon, but it was well worth the effort," said Stephanie, warming her hands on her rose-sprinkled mug. It was in the shape of a giant cup without a saucer, part of a set by a local artist as they had been shown by one of the leaflets from the hall table. They flicked through them all now as they planned a trip for the following day.

"I don't know what it is yet, Jan, but something bad is going on here," said Stephanie. "Something happened here, that's obvious. The tree seems to be involved somehow. And did you feel that energy?"

"Yes," Jan answered.

"I'm no expert, but that felt like..." Stephanie started.

"Magic!" they said, together.

They looked at each other with a worried look and finished their drinks.

"I'm going for a shower," said Jan, getting up

and placing her mug in the sink.

"OK, I'll tidy up here first. Then I'll take a bath, and we can go for a meal at the pub," Stephanie said.

"Good plan," called Jan from the hallway.

A few seconds later, Stephanie heard her voice again.

"Er, Steph, you might want to come up here!" called Jan.

Stephanie bounded up the stairs and found Jan sitting on the edge of Stephanie's bed.

"What's wrong?" Stephanie asked, a little short of breath after rushing, and her leg muscles still screaming after their walk. "Is he here again?" meaning the large, male spirit.

"No, not him. That!" said Jan, pointing towards the head of the bed.

Someone had placed a small bunch of flowers on Stephanie's pillow, a posy of tiny forget-me-nots. With five small petals of the same colour as the sky on a clear summer's day, they each had a centre of yellow, like they had been dotted with sunshine.

"I used to pick these as a child," said Stephanie, smiling.

"Me too, in *summer*...!" Jan said with a grin.

For some reason, they reminded Stephanie of the Welsh legend of Blodeuwedd, a woman made from flowers who married a man cursed to never have a human wife. She ultimately betrayed him and was turned onto an owl. Stephanie told Jan the tale.

"Who could have left them? The only other person we know of with a key is Sarah." Stephanie said.

"Unless it was someone who didn't need a key..." Jan replied. "If I remember correctly, they symbolise remembrance after death."

"I don't feel that male spirit's energy any more, so it can't have been him," said Stephanie waving her hands around in the air above the bed.

"Me either, not him or *Aunty Bessie*!" Jan added in her best attempt at a Welsh accent.

Stephanie smiled. "No, it isn't her," she agreed.

"So, as we suspected, there's more than a couple of spirits roaming the village," Jan stated.

"Yes, and one of them is targeting me," said Stephanie, with a sigh. "I suppose I should be used to that by now," she added dolefully.

"At least it makes life interesting," Jan said with a smile.

Stephanie picked up the bunch of flowers from her pillow, but as she did so they crumbled into dust on her hand and vanished without trace. The temperature in the room dropped by a few degrees and they both shivered. They had both already realised that something unnatural was going on here too; this new development was obviously something paranormal.

She frowned and Jan shook her head.

"This place is making me very uneasy," Stephanie said.

Jan nodded. "Let's get ready and go to the pub. I'm starving," she said.

She picked up a towel and headed off to the bathroom for her shower. Stephanie chose an outfit for the evening and sat in her bed looking out at the night.

As rain began to slash the windows, and the wind howled in sadness through the village, Stephanie stared out across the valley and her mind took her back to a scene from her childhood.

She must have only been about four, and it was the first Easter she could remember. She had been given a huge box containing a large chocolate egg in shiny red foil. She removed the foil and saw the egg; she remembered the smell of it, and her excitement and anticipation in thinking that the egg was a solid mass of chocolate. She ran over to show it to her father, but she had tripped and dropped it. The egg had splintered into pieces and she couldn't understand what had happened to all the chocolate that she had expected to be inside. All that was left was a bag of chocolate buttons and the fragments of the shell.

"Remember, Steffi, things aren't always as they seem," her mother had told her, putting her arms round her as she sat there on the carpet, inconsolable.

That phrase jarred within her brain, shaking at

her consciousness, like she was on the edge of grasping something. Something here wasn't as it seemed; not at all as it should be. It was hollow. Empty.

Stephanie shook off the feeling and went back downstairs to wash their mugs and put away the rest of the pack of chocolate biscuits. She read a few more of the tourist information leaflets and waited for Jan to come out of the bathroom. The muscles in her neck and shoulders were tightening and her thighs throbbed after the climb; mountain walking was not a habit she intended to pursue as a hobby. A long, hot soak in the bath would take care of all her aches and pains. But she feared that what was happening in Pentre Brân would need a lot more than a quick fix.

***

At about half past seven, Stephanie and Jan left the cottage and walked through the silent village in the direction of the pub near the crossroads. Luckily, despite a return of the rain clouds, it had been only a brief shower. The rain had stopped, and the clouds had blown over again. The evening air was bitterly cold and their breath wafted around their faces as they walked. In a few of the houses along the way, lights glowed softly behind closed curtains and blinds, but other properties were shrouded in complete darkness. They met no-one along the way.

Soon they were standing outside the pub. The lights were on and the door was closed to keep out the cold. But there was none of the noise that you would expect to hear from the only pub in the village, especially on a Saturday evening. No music or chatter came from within its walls. Stephanie and Jan looked at each other.

"I know we wanted a weekend of peace and quiet, but this is ridiculous!" said Jan.

She put her hand on the door and pushed it open. It was heavy with highly polished brass plates below the handle and at the base. The bottom panel was darkened oak, like the rest of the woodwork, and the top panel was frosted glass painted with a gold filigree pattern.

They stepped into a small entrance hall, and another similar door faced them. As Jan pushed it open, she peered inside nervously.

"It's empty," she said, stepping inside.

On the bar stood a shiny, brass bell on a wooden base, the kind that old hotels had in their reception area, the type which you pressed with the palm of your hand to call for service. Jan pressed it with relish. A middle-aged man appeared from somewhere behind the bar. He was wearing navy corduroy trousers and a check waistcoat, and he was in his shirtsleeves. He was drying and polishing a pint glass, using a traditional white tea towel with a blue stripe down the sides. He smiled when he saw them, put down the glass and the cloth, and welcomed them to the pub.

"*Noswaith dda,* good evening!" he said cheerily.

"Hello," said Jan. "Do you have any Muscadet?"

"Yes of course," replied the man. "Will that be two glasses?"

"Oh no, a bottle please," said Jan with a smile.

The man smiled back. He took a bottle of their favourite white wine from a large cooling cabinet and placed it on the bar with two sparkling glasses.

"Here for the week, are you?" asked the man.

"No, just for the weekend," said Jan. "Is it always this quiet?" she asked

"Oh, it might pick up later on," said the man with a hint of a smile.

"Not much chance of that," thought Stephanie.

Jan chatted to him a little more, and she found out that he was the landlord, as they suspected, and had lived in the village all his life.

While they chatted, Stephanie surveyed the room, which was presumably the public bar. The furniture and fixtures were all oak, with settles and sturdy tables darkened with age and marked by use. The seats had brocade cushions in shades of green, and thick, green, velvet curtains lined the windows. The surface of the bar was also brass, and it had been polished till it shone. Rows of glasses and bottles of all shapes, colours and sizes glimmered down from their shelves behind the landlord. The place was immaculate.

Horse brasses, ancient hand irons, pokers and toasting forks adorned a wide, stone fireplace to the right of the bar, facing the window. A roaring log fire had been lit, which was very inviting on such a cold night. Bilingual signage on two doors at the far end of the room indicated that one led to another bar, and the other to the toilets.

Stephanie took the glasses and sat at a table opposite the fire by the window while Jan paid and picked up the wine. The till was of the old manual variety; it was made of brass too, and covered in curls and patterns. It gave a comforting clunk as the landlord closed the drawer. Stephanie was not an antiques expert, but she guessed that it might have originated in the Victorian era; she had seen a similar one once in a period drama based in a shop.

"It's a wonder he makes any money," Jan said pouring the wine. "This place is dead, if you'll pardon the pun!"

"It's probably busier in the summer," Stephanie suggested, smiling.

"Yes, I expect you're right," Jan agreed, sipping from her glass. "Oh, I forgot to ask for a menu," she added.

"I'll get it," Stephanie said, getting up.

She walked over to the bar, picked up a leather-bound folder containing the menu, and as she did so she peered through to the room beyond, presumably the other bar. The landlord was nowhere in sight. Then her vision flickered. Just for a second, time stood still and her view of the room blurred. All she could see was a wall of darkness. She felt as if she was being sucked downwards. Down into a deep pool of nothingness. It was like she was at the bottom of a well, looking up helplessly at the world above. Then, as suddenly as her mind had been dragged from the room, she was back. She found herself gripping the bar with two hands to steady herself.

Her heart racing, she returned to where Jan was sitting with her glass half empty.

Jan noticed that her face was ashen, and she was shaking.

"What is it Steph," she asked, putting her hand on Stephanie's. "My God, your hands are freezing. Let's move closer to the fire," she said.

She picked up her glass and the bottle while Stephanie grasped her own glass tightly and sat down quickly at the nearest table to the wide stone hearth.

"You look like you've seen a... well, you know..." she said, lowering her voice. "Is there a spirit here?" Jan asked.

"No... it's not that," Stephanie began, then explained what had happened.

"That's bloody weird!" Jan said, refilling her now empty glass and topping up Stephanie's.

"I think we'd better order some food before we finish that bottle," Stephanie said with a grin, her composure returning. "I'm already feeling light-headed enough."

They chose their meal. Jan went over and called through to the other room and the landlord came and took their order. Barely twenty minutes later, they were both eating home-made steak and kidney pie, with mashed potatoes, a variety of seasonal vegetables and gravy.

"This is amazing!" Jan said.

"Yes, it's really good," agreed Stephanie.

For dessert, Jan chose apple crumble and cream, and Stephanie had treacle pudding with custard. They could barely move by the time they had finished.

"My compliments to the chef," Jan said, when the landlord came to collect their dishes.

"That would be me," he said with a proud smile. "I'm glad you enjoyed it."

"I'm going to the ladies," said Jan, after he had disappeared behind the bar again.

"OK, I'm going to take a look at what's in that other room," said Stephanie.

They walked to the end of the room and Jan took the door on the right while Stephanie opened the one to the left. A small corridor led to some stairs and on the left was a door saying *BAR PREIFAT*: a private bar.

She opened it, and inside she found a small room containing a long settle-type bench with three round, oak tables and a few hard-backed chairs. Each seat was covered with a plump, red velvet cushion. The room was what might be termed a snug, a small, cosy seating area possibly reserved just for local customers. It was also, as expected, empty. It had a little corner bar, and when she looked behind it to the left, she could see the room that she had just come from. To the right, she could just make out a kitchen where the landlord was washing dishes. This time, she experienced nothing out of the ordinary. She caught sight of Jan returning to the main bar and went back to join her.

She told Jan what she found, unremarkable though it was. What she had seen earlier made no sense, just like everything else in this strange little village. She was becoming used to receiving visions and cryptic messages from spirits in need of her help. But this felt different. The messages she was receiving felt more like a personal warning. Leave, or else…

***

Ten o'clock came and went, and so did a second bottle of wine. Warm, relaxed and comforted by good food and alcohol, they decided to go back to the cottage and have an early night. It had been a busy day. With the tiredness that came from travelling, a long walk and being up late the night before, they both needed a good night's sleep. They thanked the landlord again, said goodnight, and went on their way.

They heard the bolt being shot on the pub door almost as soon as they left, which seemed strange. Stephanie turned back and was surprised to see that all the lights were out. In fact, the only lights in the whole village came from the street lights and the smiling full moon. She looked up at the window, but this time no faces watched them as they stood there. None that could be seen, anyway. The air was very cold.

She mentioned these developments to Jan who, having consumed most of the wine, was currently oblivious to any of the potential implications.

They soon arrived back at the cottage, shivering, and decided to have hot chocolate before bed. Stephanie had brought their favourite brand and prepared it while Jan changed into her pink satin pyjamas and matching dressing-gown. She topped it with some tiny marshmallows and grated chocolate that she had also brought with her.

Realising that her clothing was a little too thin for a cottage with no central heating, Jan turned on an electric fire and found a blanket. Then they drank the hot chocolate and chatted by the glow of lamplight. Stephanie thought it was best not to try to discuss what had happened at the pub, or to attempt to make sense of anything until they had slept. So, they reminisced about school days and past holidays until Jan began to doze holding her empty mug. Stephanie shook her awake, put the mugs in the sink and followed her up to their room.

Jan was asleep as soon as her head hit the pillow. Wearing brushed cotton pyjamas fit for Welsh weather, Stephanie snuggled into her cosy bed, and soon she drifted off to sleep too, oblivious to the unnatural chill that had settled all around them and the small girl who stood by her bed, stroking her hair as she slept.

***

Stephanie was dreaming that she was walking down a country lane. It was the middle of summer. The sky was forget-me-not blue, the sun was a glowing yellow ball in the sky and the air burned hot. Then the scene changed, and she was climbing a familiar mountain path amid lush, green grass sprinkled with buttercups and daisies. Clumps of daffodils sprouted here and there.

Soon she found herself standing before the wishing tree. With tender loving care, she placed a long, pink ribbon on a low branch, wound it round three times and tied it into a bow. She wiped a fallen tear from her cheek. At the base of the tree she lay a small teddy bear, then she turned to walk back down to the village. But as she rounded the bend in the path, the village wasn't there. All she could see was the grass, the fields and the river. The rest was just blackness. A voice was calling.

"Sioned," it said, "it's time to go!"

***

Stephanie woke up. She felt disoriented until she remembered where she was. She looked at her phone on the bedside table; it said nine o'clock.

"Jan," she began, turning over to face the door to tell her what she had just seen.

Jan's bed was empty. She could hear the shower and something that loosely passed for singing coming from the bathroom. She smiled. Jan hadn't been blessed with the best of voices, but she sang like she did everything else: with great enthusiasm. Also, plenty of volume.

Sunlight streamed in through the window from a cloudless sky. The air was chilly, so Stephanie jumped out of bed, put on her dressing gown and rushed downstairs to put on the kettle and the electric fire. Soon Jan appeared at the kitchen table in designer jeans and a new sweatshirt. She was freshly scrubbed, dressed and made -up with shiny, perfectly straightened hair. Stephanie made her a coffee and waved her hand towards toast made from the last of the bread. The local butter lay next to it, alongside tiny catering pots of jam and marmalade which she found in a cupboard.

"Help yourself," she said.

"Thanks Steph," said Jan, grinning. "Did you sleep well?" she asked.

"Yes thanks, must be the mountain air," Stephanie said. "Apart from one odd dream, which I don't think *was* a dream…"

Stephanie explained about the girl called Sioned (which she explained her was Welsh for Janet) and related the dream about the wishing tree and the missing village. It didn't seem like a dream, more like a memory. Sioned's memory.

"It just gets weirder and weirder!" said Jan, crunching her toast. "Who is Sioned do you think? What did she look like?"

"I don't know. I felt like I was looking through Sioned's eyes. Like I *was* Sioned, and I was placing gifts in memory of someone. Maybe a child, her child," said Stephanie.

"Do you think it might be Sioned who left you the flowers?" Jan asked.

"I think you're right, the energy felt similar," Stephanie said.

"I'll check online to see if I can find anything," said Jan.

Jan took her phone out of her back pocket and switched it on. Then she frowned.

"Damn, no signal," she said. "Try yours, you're on a different network."

Stephanie turned on at her phone, and she had no signal either.

"It must be because of the mountains," Jan said.

"Not much use to us though," said Stephanie. "And a little worrying if we can't call for backup."

It occurred to them both that with all that had had happened and their agreement to avoid their devices, they hadn't even noticed that their phones had probably been out of service since they arrived, or that the cottage had no landline. Stephanie reminded Jan about the landlord bolting the pub door, and the lack of lights at ten o'clock at night. Jan had to agree that it seemed unusual.

"OK, we need to figure this out, and fast," said Stephanie, "then get the hell out of this freaky village for good! Without a phone, we have no way to call for help if we need it, and I don't really fancy spending another night here, even if they have a great pub with fabulous food! If something nasty decides to attack us…"

"OK, no need to spell it out," Jan said.

They had both dealt with enough 'nasties' in recent months to know that this might not end well.

"I think we're dealing with some sort of mass tragedy," said Jan. "Finding out what it was might be the only way to work out what Sioned wants."

"I agree," said Stephanie. "If the wishing tree is any indication, a lot of people died here, maybe together. The ribbons and offerings we saw all looked quite recent and in the same condition. No ageing or weather damage."

"I think we need to start asking questions around the village," said Jan, "and find out where Sarah lives. We have her number, but we can't ring her, so we'll just have to go looking for her. Grab your coat, Steph!"

"Let me finish my tea first!" said Stephanie. "I have a feeling it's going to be another long day."

***

At half past ten they left the cottage, wrapped up against the chill wind in thick winter coats, scarves and gloves. They had decided to cross the road and work their way up to the crossroads then back down the other side to the cottage, ending up at the tea-room, for what Jan hoped would be a decent cup of coffee. Their first port of call was the supermarket, and it was open. But Jan's eyes had already drifted once more to the sweet shop next door. Stephanie took one look at her pleading face not unlike a like a child's and decided it was futile to argue. But to

Jan's great disappointment, the sweet shop was closed, so Stephanie dragged her away from the window and back to the supermarket.

The shop was empty apart from a motherly woman behind a counter at the far end. She was rearranging a display of tinned boiled sweets, the kind that came covered in icing sugar. Jan, having missed out on replenishing her rations of locally made fudge, pounced on them with glee, and began sorting through the flavours while Stephanie engaged the woman in conversation.

"Hello, beautiful day," started Stephanie.

"Yes, *cariad,* it is that," said the woman with a beaming smile, and cold, dark eyes. Stephanie knew that *cariad* meant "darling", but the shopkeeper's words didn't quite match up with the way she was looking at her.

"We were wondering if you could tell us where Sarah Jenkins lives," she asked with a smile. "We're renting Tŷ Nant and we need to ask her something. There's no phone signal…" she said, her voice drifting off.

"Sorry, no!" said the woman firmly, glaring at Stephanie.

"OK, sorry to have bothered you," she replied, a little taken aback.

"How rude!" Stephanie thought.

"Oh, no trouble at all," answered the woman with a smile.

She went over to the chiller cabinet and picked up a pint of milk, surprised to see that it was in a glass bottle, like the one they had at the cottage. It hadn't occurred to her before. It was rare these days, but she found it quaint and homely, and it reminded her of her childhood.

She was getting nowhere with her questioning, she paid for the milk and Jan's sweets, and they left the shop.

"That didn't help much," said Stephanie.

"Oh, I don't know, I have sweets for the journey home," said Jan triumphantly, "and we have fresh milk."

Stephanie had to admit that she had a point.

When they reached the shop selling ladieswear, they found that it was also closed.

"Let's take a break from the questioning, and

have a look around the streets we didn't visit yesterday," said Jan.

Stephanie agreed. The morning was bright, and the sunlight was warm between the gusts of cold wind that whistled down the street. They reached the crossroads and took the route to the left, up the lane just before the pub. They came to the terrace of three stone cottages which they had seen the day before. These had gardens at the front; the way they clung to the side of the mountain would leave no room for anything at the rear. A bilingual sign told them that the street was aptly named *Lon - y - Mynydd*: Mountain Lane.

Here too the windows stared back at them like closed eyelids, with their curtains firmly shut. The wind whooshed past their ears, and the crows called to each other in the crisp morning air, echoing once more down the valley.

"Crows are a portent of death, aren't they?" asked Stephanie.

"Don't remind me!" said Jan, pulling her scarf tighter round her throat. "This whole village feels like a graveyard, if you ask me."

"I'm sorry," said Stephanie, feeling guilty for having brought her friend to such a dismal location. Their break was turning out to be less than restful. Jan realised what she meant.

"It's not your fault, it looked wonderful online," said Jan with a grin. "And you know I love a good mystery."

Stephanie smiled back. At the end of the lane was a gate with a footpath leading to a bench. Beyond that was a fence next to a sheer drop down the mountain side. They could walk no further, so they went back to the bench and sat down.

"Sweet?" asked Jan, offering Stephanie the tin she had bought in the supermarket. Stephanie nodded and thanked her. Taking off her right glove she took a red one: strawberry-flavoured.

Jan took off one glove too and picked up a green sweet, which turned out to her delight to be apple flavoured which she loved, not lime which she hated. They both soon replaced their gloves; the seat was quite exposed to the elements and the mountain air was freezing.

"These sweets are great!" she said with enthusiasm, putting the lid back firmly on the tin and popping it into her bag.

"So is the view," said Stephanie.

They sat for a while, surveying the landscape. From that point, they could see for miles. Green rolling hills; farms and woods, and the wide river rushing along in the bottom of the valley far below them. As it tumbled over rocks on its inescapable journey towards the sea, light sparkled as it reflected the sunshine and the blue of the February sky. Forget-me-not blue.

Stephanie was shaken out of her reverie by the reminder of what they had to do. She didn't know why, but she knew that Sioned was depending on them. It was far too cold to sit still for long, so they stood up and turned back towards the village.

When they reached the crossroads, Stephanie had a funny feeling, like she was being watched.

There on the top of a signpost sat a massive crow. It stared at her intently with its beady, black eyes. She turned away and walked off, but whenever she looked back,

its gaze seemed to be following her as she walked down the lane. Its eyes looked almost human. She shook off the fanciful notion. Her brain was on high alert, and her imagination must have been playing tricks on her.

They followed the road which seemed to be leading behind the cottage where they were staying and slightly uphill, no doubt affording the inhabitants undisturbed views of the valley. There they found four newer properties to the left of the road: two semi-detached houses, a small bungalow, and a detached property right on the end. As expected, blinds and shutters covered every window, and the road was as quiet as the grave.

The unremarkable red, brick-built, semi-detached houses were built in 1953, according to an engraved stone plaque situated below the eaves, right in the centre of the two. The quaint bungalow was also made of brick and covered in climbing rose bushes. They were bare now, but they would have been ablaze with colour in mid-summer. Stephanie would have loved to see that; her mother had loved roses, and she shared her passion.

They came to the detached house which was quite a large, double-fronted, villa style property and set back a bit from the road. Opposite, they could see the wall which they were certain was the boundary of the back garden of their holiday cottage. Jan, being taller, stood on her tiptoes and peered over the wall to check, and they were right.

The house was a grim place. Dark and foreboding, it gave off an aura of desolation. Stained glass windows in shades of blue stood either side of the doorway, shining like watchful eyes as sunbeams bounced off them. They approached the house and to their surprise the front door was slightly ajar. It was painted a glossy black and had a brass door knocker in the shape of a lion's head. For some reason, it struck Stephanie as being very familiar. A thought took shape somewhere at the back of her brain, taunting her to remember. Then before she could grasp it, Jan spoke, and it was gone.

"Hello, anyone home?" she called into the darkness inside the house.

Jan held the door with one hand while rapping firmly with the brass door knocker. Stephanie felt compelled to go inside.

Jan's voice echoed down the hallway and silence

was the only reply. Victorian style, diagonal tiles in red and black adorned the floor of the hallway, with a seemingly endless parallel border of white. They drew Stephanie's gaze inside; on and on until they disappeared into the darkness within. So familiar. She felt like she was being taken along with them and felt unsteady on her feet. She stepped inside and became instantly dizzy. Her knees were weak, she felt as if the walls were moving, sucking her inside. Her surroundings started to swirl. It felt as if the house was collapsing in on her.

"Steph, come back," Jan said, clutching the shiny door. "Don't go any further!"

They were both so sensitive that they picked up on energy and this house was thick with it. Jan obviously didn't want Stephanie to be affected. She felt someone tug at her arm, then she found herself back outside leaning against the front door.

"Are you OK?" asked a Jan. "You looked like you were going to fall over."

"I almost did!" Stephanie said. "Strong energy," she added, taking a bottle of water from her pocket and drinking half of it in quick, successive gulps.

"Yes, very bad. We shouldn't go in there," Jan warned.

"Let me try again," said Stephanie, confident that she would be able to fare better this time.

"No! We should go," said Jan.

Jan looked so worried that Stephanie didn't argue. Jan put an arm around her friend and guided away from the house and didn't let go until she was sure she was steady on her feet again.

"That was…" Stephanie started.

"Odd? Weird? Strange? Absolutely! Whatever you want to call it, this place has it in bucket-loads. I don't know about you, but I feel like Alice in Wonderland…"

"Down the rabbit hole. Yes!" Stephanie replied. "Shall we go back to the cottage?" she asked.

"No, I want answers!" said Jan defiantly, as the water and the fresh air began helping them both regain their energy. "We need to find out what we can from the villagers."

Since they were children Stephanie had never seen anything get the better of Jan. She was strong, determined and resilient. Stephanie smiled. It was good to know there was something in this village that she could rely on, and she knew without doubt that Jan would never let her down.

There was no exit to the main road, just a bare meadow sloping up onto the mountain. They left the houses and turned back towards the crossroads. The road to the next village was swathed in fog like before. Turning back into the village, they walked back down the same side of the road as their cottage. By this time, Stephanie had finished her water and was fully recovered. Spirit energy had a habit of causing the psychically attuned to become rather dehydrated.

***

When they reached the village, they were pleased to see that the shop with all manner of camping and walking gear was open for business. They stepped inside and were met with an Aladdin's cave of treasure for the traveller, camper, climber and weekend hiker. Guides, scouts and birdwatching enthusiasts were also well catered for. It was surprising how much stock was contained in such a small space, and the effect was more than a little claustrophobic. The owner was alone, a jolly, ruddy-faced man who looked like he had been poured into an under-sized set of camouflage gear. He had an air of authority which came from his years of obvious experience; they felt confident that anyone purchasing from his shop could do so safe in the knowledge that he knew just what they needed, and where to find it in the murky depths of his over-stuffed establishment.

"*Bore da*! How can I help you, ladies?" he said with a grin as wide as his round face.

"Morning!" said Jan. "We're trying to find out a little about the history of this beautiful village, and I was wondering if you…"

"No, no, no. Not my area of expertise," said the man in a broad Welsh accent, looking horror-struck at the very suggestion.

"In that case, could you maybe tell us where Sarah Jenkins lives?" asked Stephanie.

"I'm sorry, no. No, I can't do that," said the man,

shaking his head vehemently.

Then he looked outside to see if anyone was there and stepped closer to Stephanie.

"Leave now, while you still can!" he whispered with a nod, not threateningly but with a genuine air of deep concern.

Then he disappeared behind the counter into a back room and slammed the door.

"OK then!" said Jan, raising her eyebrows and placing her hands on her hips.

Stephanie frowned back at her and they hurriedly left the shop.

"What the hell was that all about?" Jan said.

"I have no idea, but this place is starting to creep me out!" said Stephanie.

Another empty shop, another dead end, and a direct warning, this time from the living. They weren't imagining it. They had been told to leave the village; twice. What had been left unsaid was that someone obviously didn't want them poking around in their business, asking questions, or finding Sarah. But who, and what were they hiding?

***

"Have you noticed that there don't seem to be any animals here? No cats or dogs anywhere, and I haven't seen any birds either, apart from crows," said Stephanie as they walked.

"No, I hadn't," Jan said. "But I'm not really an animal person."

Stephanie was momentarily reminded of Maisy and was struck by the pang of guilt that she always felt after leaving her. Then she cast her mind back to the walk that they had taken earlier. She realised that she hadn't seen any other creatures either, not in the village, or on the mountain.

"And there are no children out playing," Stephanie added.

"It's freezing, Steph," Jan said.

The weather was admittedly cold, but it was dry, and children could easily be let out to run around in the fresh air in warm clothing. No sounds of children's laughter could be heard coming from any of the properties. No babies cried. There was also no sign of toys, apart from by the wishing tree.

"Or cars. We haven't seen any vehicles either. Something else to add to the list of weirdness, I suppose," Stephanie added.

Jan gave a shadow of a resigned smile and a shrug of her shoulders.

Suddenly, as they walked along, they heard a church bell ringing loudly.

"I love the sound of church bells," said Jan.

It was a comforting reminder of her childhood.

"Me too," said Stephanie. "But Jan, we've been around the whole of this village and it doesn't have a church. And there's no chapel either."

"You're right," said Jan.

She was aware that it was usually only churches that had bells. But one thing she remembered from her previous visits to Wales was that most villages had at least one chapel, often a few of different denominations, and this village had no places of worship whatsoever.

"Maybe the sound is coming from a nearby

village," Jan suggested.

"Then why does it sound so close?" Stephanie asked.

The nearest village was several miles away although it was possible that it might have carried down the valley. But they both doubted that it would sound that loud.

They looked at each other, Jan shrugged her shoulders and they walked on. Each ring shook the ground and resonated on their ears, in their heads. Like a large, pounding hammer clanging against a huge anvil, it shook their brains and jarred all their senses. It was as if the ground below their feet was shuddering, and they felt like they were swaying with its rhythm. Stephanie's vision started to blur and the mountains and shops, houses and gardens all shimmered as if they were covered in a blue light. Then the sound stopped. It was as if the world had righted itself.

"A death knoll," thought Stephanie.

"Let's go inside," said Jan, determinedly.

They were standing outside the tea-room and gift shop, so they went in and sat at a small round table near the window. Again, they were the only customers. They took off their gloves and coats. Stephanie took her scarf off, but Jan unwound hers and let Stephanie stared at it; to her it seemed to hang loosely round her neck like a lank, knitted snake.

"I need to get a grip!" she thought. This village, this situation, was getting to her more than she cared to admit.

The tea-shop had white, glossy, painted furniture, and the curtains were white with sprigs of yellow primroses and matching tie-backs. The crockery had a pattern of bright, yellow daffodils, and the sunny effect was completed by tablecloths in the tiny checks of yellow and white gingham. It all looked fresh and clean, like a spring morning, and it felt cosy and welcoming on such a cold day.

A woman in her twenties rushed over, introduced herself as Gwen and hovered while they looked at the short, but tasty, menu. To Jan's delight, they sold filter coffee and home-made cakes, so she ordered a large cappuccino with chocolate fudge cake, and Stephanie chose a latte with a slice of carrot cake. They chatted amongst themselves while their order was prepared and decided to take their time here, enjoy their coffee and cake and size up the waitress to decide on the best approach.

"She could be our last hope of finding out anything of significance," said Stephanie.

"Yes, for now anyway. But we can always go back to the pub tonight. The landlord seemed like he would know a thing or two about what goes on in the village," Jan said.

"Definitely. Landlords have a reputation for being a good source of local knowledge, also people tend to use them as a sort of confidant. A pub is often the social hub of a village. At least in a normal village where there are people who socialise, but this could hardly be described as a normal village!" Stephanie whispered the last part and Jan grinned.

Gwen brought their cakes and returned soon after with the coffees; it all lived up to expectation.

"Is it just me, or have you noticed how everything in this village is just perfect?" asked Jan. "I mean, the service, the food, even my love for fudge, apple sweets not lime, and the pub selling our favourite wine…? What a lovely place!"

Stephanie thought about it. It was perfect. Then she looked up at the counter and caught the waitress looking at her. Just for a second her face changed. The flesh fell off, the uniform was replaced by a white shroud and Stephanie found herself looking at a skull. In an instant, she was back to normal. Stephanie gasped.

"What's wrong?" Jan asked, looking worried.

"Everything!" said Stephanie. "You're right, it's all too perfect. Look around you, really look hard."

They both looked at the counter. At first, it looked normal, then it seemed to twitch in and out of focus. As Stephanie watched, the curtains began to fade and became tattered rags. The white of the walls and furniture turned grey. The remnants of their cake became mouldy and crawling with maggots. She blinked and shook her head, and everything was as it had been, bright and cheerful. Jan obviously saw it too because Stephanie saw the shock on her face.

"We're leaving!" Stephanie said.

Throwing money onto the saucer containing the bill, she ran out of the tea-room with Jan close behind.

"Wait! said Gwen.

Then as they slammed the door, they heard her call after them, "I'm sorry."

They stood on the street staring at each other in horror as the reality of their situation hit them.

"It's starting to make sense now," said Jan.

"Yes. Whatever is going on here is either magical or paranormal in origin," said Stephanie, "because none of what we've seen since we arrived in Pentre Brân has been real!"

***

"We have to leave," said Stephanie when they arrived back at the cottage.

"But what about Sioned?" asked Jan. "If we go now, we'll never find out what she wants or how to help her."

"To hell with Sioned! What about us, Jan? We have no clue what we're dealing with, or what they want. We also have no contact with the outside world. I think we should go upstairs, pack as fast as we can, and get out of here while we still can."

Stephanie's instincts told her that the spirit she knew as Sioned, and maybe others too, needed their help. But at the same time, she knew that she was right to walk away. They were alone, and at the mercy of whatever was putting on this macabre show for their benefit. Just then, there was a knock at the door. Jan went to the small window and glanced outside towards the doorway.

"It's Sarah!" she said and Stephanie went to open the door.

"I hear you've been looking for me," said Sarah, her face serious.

"Yes, please come in," replied Stephanie.

Sarah stepped inside and followed Stephanie into the living-room. As she did so, the spirit of the woman that they knew as her Aunty Bessie appeared beside her. Jan looked at Stephanie

"Are you the one responsible for all this?" asked Jan sternly.

"I am, and I'm sorry," said Bessie.

"Why is everyone saying that?" yelled Jan.

"Because once you come to this village, you can never leave," said Bessie, smiling once more. But this time her eyes became dark, all pupil, like pools of black ink.

"But it's alright, we will look after you well," said Sarah.

The two women both leaned their heads towards one shoulder and smiled. Stephanie's stomach lurched in panic.

"Now, you listen to me," she began, "we have no intention of staying…!"

"You have no choice, *cariad,*" said Bessie.

Suddenly a young woman appeared out of nowhere and took Stephanie and Jan by the hand. The next thing they knew, they were on the mountain near the wishing tree.

"It's OK, she can't set foot here. This is a sacred place!" said the woman, smiling at them kindly.

Stephanie had already recognised the feel of her energy. It was soft and pure, wafting around them, bathing them in light like the gentle rays of the sun at dawn when it first rises over the horizon to bless the day. She was mid-twenties with straight, long, blonde hair and sky blue eyes.

"Sioned?" she asked. The woman nodded.

"Please can you tell us what's going on?" she asked. "Nothing has made sense since we arrived here."

"It's all because of Bessie," said Sioned. "She wants to keep us here, earthbound, to feed her fantasy of a perfect village. But the village is long gone!"

"What do you mean, gone?" asked Stephanie, looking shocked.

"Where we're standing, this mountain and the high ground around us, this is all that's left of Pentre Brân."

"I don't understand," said Jan. "What happened to the village?"

"It would be better if I showed you," said Sioned,

taking their hands once more.

Instantly they saw what Sioned wanted to show them. It was a beautiful summer day; trees were filled with singing birds, the air rich with brightly coloured butterflies and dragonflies. The grass was like a carpet patterned with daisies, buttercups and forget-me-nots. Everyone was going about their business, the shops and cafe were full, and an open-air market was underway in the main street. Vehicles streamed in and out of the village, tourists wandered happily up and down and children played in their gardens, or in a small park which stood on the edge of the village just beyond the crossroads. It was a thriving community.

Then the scene changed. They heard a bell, ringing in a church that stood at the end of the main street opposite the pub. Its bells were clanging with urgency, giving out a warning. There were no more cars; the streets were deserted save for a handful of people outside *Tŷ* Nant. There was a woman standing defiantly in the street with her hands on her hips: Bessie. They picked up on a conversation; Sioned was Bessie's granddaughter. She pleaded with her, her own small daughter clinging to her hand.

Still Bessie shook her head and pushed Sioned away. She finally went into her house and slammed the door. Sioned ran to the car where Sarah waited at the wheel as the bell stopped ringing. Sarah was Sioned's mother.

Stephanie and Jan looked on in horror as the scene unfolded in their minds.

It started as a trickle, just a slow widening of the river, then it crept higher and higher. Sioned looked on in panic, frozen to the spot. Sarah fumbled with the door handle, trying to open the door, but Sioned's body was blocking it. She opened a window and shouted at Sioned, trying to get her attention. But Sioned just stood, wide-eyed in terror, holding her small daughter close, her gaze fixed on the water that was fast approaching, like someone had opened a floodgate higher in the valley. With a rumble and a whooshing sound, the water rose higher as a torrent came rushing down. The valley was being deliberately flooded.

The river had risen steadily behind Sioned while she had begged her grandmother to leave the cottage. It was already too late when she realised that her feet were wet. Unable to open the car door against the pressure of the rising river, Sioned screamed as she swept her child up in her arms and tried to run. But it was like wading through treacle. Sarah was trapped inside the car, unable to open the doors as the filthy water seeped in. She tried desperately to close the window, but water full of silt churned up from the bottom of the river poured inside, lashing at her face, filling her mouth. It rose higher and higher until all air was replaced; until her death mask stared out at her daughter as she turned in terror and tried to get away.

A man pushed his way to them, chest deep in the swell, half-wading, half swimming. It was the large man who had tried to warn them in their bedroom. He tried to help Sioned and her daughter, grasping at the child as she was dragged from her mother's arms. He was as helpless as she was. The child was gone. Soon the water, now a raging torrent, took him too, and Sioned's voice could be heard still screaming for her child until water filled her lungs. She was pulled along by the flood and sucked down. Deep down into the muddy water where death claimed her too.

As the vision faded, they could see Bessie's

terrified face in the window of the cottage as she witnessed the scene, and a silent scream froze on her lips as the water filled her gaping mouth and rose up over her head.

The roaring swell eventually subsided, and a lake formed. A new reservoir. The valley was calm. The village had vanished: it lay buried under the water. It wasn't meant to happen like that; the company who had flooded the river had thought that everyone had left. But a handful of stragglers and one or two residents determined to stay to the last had been caught out. It was never disclosed; covered up in the name of profit.

But Sioned knew only too well what had happened. She stood with Stephanie and Jan on the top of the mountain by the wishing tree, all looking out at the vast expanse of water that surrounded them. It was an idyllic scene which hid a tale of death. They turned to her, three women sharing a terrible secret with tears flowing freely down their cheeks. Her forget-me-nots were a symbol of remembrance, and a reminder of the past before the flood when her little girl was still alive. They understood now what she wanted; that their story be told. Before that could happen, there was more that they had yet to discover, understand and put right. But first, they had to leave Pentre Brân.

***

Stephanie and Jan were back in the living room of the cottage. Sioned, Sarah and Bessie were nowhere in sight. They looked at each other.

"How awful!" said Stephanie wiping her eyes. "Those poor people."

"Yes," said Jan as she went into the kitchen to put the kettle on. "It's hard to believe that anyone would get away with that," she said, walking back into the living room.

"We saw it with our own eyes, Jan. Don't you believe it?" Stephanie said, her sympathy turning to anger.

"Oh, I believe it," Jan replied. "But how are we going to prove it?"

It all seemed impossible. Yet at the same time it made sense. The jigsaw pieces were starting to fall together in Stephanie's mind. The village of Pentre Brân was an illusion constructed from someone else's memory; apparently, it was created by Bessie. She had made it as perfect as she could to appeal to Stephanie and Jan, to try to keep them there.

"First, we need to get out of this village," said Stephanie. "You make the coffee and make it strong!"

Stephanie went upstairs and started putting her belongings into her weekend bag. Soon Jan joined her and they drank the coffee while they finished packing. It was almost one o'clock by this time. They decided that they could stop for lunch on the way and be back in Marlin well before dark. They went downstairs, making sure they had left nothing behind and rushed out to the car, leaving the house keys on the hall table and the door open as they had found it.

But when they got into the car, it wouldn't start. The battery was dead.

"Damn!" said Jan.

"I don't remember leaving the lights on," said Stephanie.

"You didn't," said Jan. "It's been drained of charge, probably by Bessie."

They both checked their phones, which still had

no signal. They took their bags back into the cottage and put them in the hall.

Then they saw Sioned standing in the living-room, looking out over the valley.

"You can't leave," she said. "It's tomorrow you see, the anniversary. She wants you here."

"Who, Bessie? The anniversary of the flood?" asked Stephanie.

"Yes," Sioned replied, still staring out of the window. "You need to break the spell and you can only do that tomorrow, but if you fail, you can never leave. Just like the others," she said, turning to face them.

As they stared at her in horror, she faded to nothing before their eyes. They had so many questions and, so it appeared, very little time to find answers.

"What are we doing to do?" asked Stephanie, sitting on the sofa with a soft thump as her legs became weak and the seriousness of their situation dawned on her.

"Take a deep breath, and go over everything we know about bloody Bessie and the village that time forgot!" said Jan, flopping into an armchair in her exasperation.

Jan hated being backed into a corner. She looked angry, and when she was angry, her brain fired on all cylinders. Stephanie had to smile.

"OK!" she replied. "Let's start at the beginning. Bessie wants us to stay, so she isn't going to harm us, and that's a bonus in my book!"

"Agreed!" replied Jan. "She's obviously using magic to make it seem like we are in Pentre Brân as it used to be before the flood, or her version of it without children animals or cars. And the only people we've seen have been Sarah, the shopkeepers, tea room waitress and pub landlord."

"Sarah!" said Stephanie. "She's dead too. How didn't we pick up on that? And the others probably are too. Why wouldn't the spirit of Sioned be living here too, and her daughter?"

"I don't know," said Jan. "I expect Sioned probably wants no part of it," she added.

"But the other people, are they dead too? I didn't sense any energy from them and they seemed very much alive to me," Stephanie replied.

"Exactly. I have a theory and you're not going to like it. Steph." Jan said looking worried.

A pang of fear grabbed Stephanie. She dreaded what Jan was about to say because she thought she knew what that was.

"They could be spirits of other people who drowned, or…." Jan paused, a look of disgust on her face. "Or they could be people like us who she's trapped here too! In their minds, in her vision. People she's forced to stay and act out her sick charade!"

"Oh, my God, Jan!" Stephanie said. "How long have they been here do you think? We don't know how long ago the village was flooded. Or how many people she's tricked into visiting here. Well, if Sioned wants us to end this, she needs to give us answers. We can't do this alone," she added.

They both fell silent, lost in thought for a few moments.

"There is one other option," said Jan with an expression of pure horror. "We could already be dead like the others."

***

A few moments had passed since Jan dropped her bombshell. They tried to make sense of their situation, something which was becoming more difficult by the minute.

"I don't feel dead, Steph," said Jan as they tried to rationalise their situation.

"How would you know?" Stephanie replied, in amusement.

She was half-joking yet hoping that Jan could reassure her that they were, in fact, very much alive. Jan frowned.

"Sorry. I know this isn't funny," said Stephanie.

"No, it isn't. All joking aside, we really don't know what's going on, do we?" Jan said.

She had a point. "How is she managing to keep us in this illusion? Is it magic? Is it all in our heads? Maybe we're asleep. Where the hell are we, for one thing… did we ever leave Marlin?" Stephanie asked, starting to make sense of it all.

Stephanie stood up and gazed out over the valley.

"Did we ever leave Marlin?" she thought. Her

words echoed round and round in her head.

"Of course, we left Marlin. Don't you remember? We stopped for lunch at that pizza place in Exeter that you like," Jan insisted.

"No, we didn't!" Stephanie exclaimed. "We had lunch at the services not long after we crossed the Severn Bridge."

She looked at Jan and just for a split-second her face twitched out of focus.

"What does it matter! We have better things to worry about!" Jan said.

Suddenly she remembered her own words, not an hour before.

"None of what we've seen since we arrived in Pentre Brân has been real!"

Did that also include Jan?

The more she looked at her friend, the more she began to doubt that Jan was Jan, or that Jan was even there. She remembered some other thoughts from the past twenty-four hours.

"It's all too perfect," Jan had said.

What better way to make her think she had left Marlin than to make her think Jan had persuaded her. Jan had never been to Wales before so this village must be one based on her own memories.

Forget-me-nots from her childhood. Church bells from her childhood. These were snippets of her life taken from her own mind. Whatever was going on, someone was trying to tell her something. Helping her find a way out, maybe? So someone wanted her to stay, and someone else was trying to persuade her to leave.

She looked again at Jan, sitting in the armchair nearest the door. Jan was the one who had wanted to stay; why was she keeping her here? Her addled brain began making connections. Stephanie realised something; whoever wanted her to stay in this village had been somehow using their friendship as a weapon, and that was unforgivable. But how were they doing it? Jan would never willingly agree to do something to harm her. Was it magic? Then the truth hit her.

"You're not real," she said suddenly.

"What do you mean?" asked Jan, standing up and walking towards her.

"GO!" Stephanie yelled.

Jan, or whatever Jan had been, crumbled to dust before her eyes just like the bunch of forget-me-nots that she had found on her bed. As she vanished, she whispered two words.

"I'm sorry!"

***

Stephanie stood there, alone in the cottage, knowing now that this was all an intricate illusion. Her thoughts were all over the place. The village was fake, as was Jan. She needed to find a way out of this. But how could she possibly escape when the chances were that she was trapped within her own mind?

"GO HOME!" said the voice of Lucas in her head.

"I would if I could!" she replied out loud. "How, Lucas? Tell me how!"

Tears filled her eyes.

"REMEMBER!" said Lucas.

Stephanie paced up and down, looking at the walls around her as they twitched and shuddered. It felt like the house was like a hall of mirrors at a funfair and she had become hopelessly lost. But what had been reflected back at her what was what someone else wanted her to see.

"Home," she said, pondering for a moment.

That word had huge implications. Safety, security. Love. Marlin was her home now, and it seemed a long way away. Then she remembered something: until she moved to Marlin, no matter where she had lived, home had always meant the house that she grew up in; the house where she had first felt loved.

"The house!" she thought. She could sense that Lucas was smiling.

The memories flooded back. The house with the Victorian floor tiles that stood behind Tŷ Nant was identical to her childhood home on the outskirts of Bristol; large, double-fronted, villa style, and set back from the road. That was where Lucas was telling her to go. How could she have forgotten? She also remembered how Jan, or something resembling Jan, had tried to stop her going back into the house before. The hallway had been full of energy, but that energy had been good not bad. That's why whoever was mimicking Jan couldn't go inside. *That* house, that hallway was her way home.

She stepped outside. Storm-clouds were gathering overhead, and the wind was rising; more illusion to deter her from leaving. She realised that it was a long way through the village and back around to the house, and that Bessie and the others might try to stop her. She needed a shortcut.

"This is MY vision now," she said aloud, to whoever was listening.

She was in control. She had sent the false Jan away and she would make a shortcut.

She went into the kitchen and unlocked the back door. She stood facing a brick wall.

"This isn't real!" she told herself, and it vanished.

She found herself in a small paved courtyard with three steps to an upper patio. That patio ended at the wall that backed onto the house. Her family home. She ran up the steps. She held out her hands and touched the wall. A small, black metal gate appeared, and she pushed it open. In front of her was the house. As she rushed towards it, Sioned appeared.

"Please don't go," she pleased. "You need to stay and make things right..."

"I will," said Stephanie. "I promise. But I can't do it here."

Sioned vanished and Stephanie ran as fast as she could to the black door, still ajar, and pushed it open. Instead of ominous and threatening like before, now it felt warm and safe. Inside it was still dark, but wall lights lit as she walked past them. She went past the front room on the right and saw the familiar staircase facing her. On the right was the door to the living room and beyond that she knew she would find the kitchen. But she had no time for a tour. She had one destination in mind, the place where she had always felt safe.

She ran upstairs to where her bedroom used to be, one of four, and stepped inside. It was exactly as she had left it when she moved out at eighteen to go to university. She had never lived there again. Her purple floral comforter lay on the bed. The white walls and furniture, lilac carpet and floral curtains were as they should be. She was home.

Stephanie was overcome with overwhelming

tiredness. Her small, beloved teddy bear lay on the pillow, the one that had been a gift from her Dad when she had the measles at the age of five. He still wore the navy-blue shorts that her mother had made for him. She picked him up and hugged him, then holding him close like she had as a child, she lay down on the bed and fell asleep, soaking him with tears as she had done so often before.

***

"Steph, wake up," called a voice.

She recognised the voice: it was Jan. Stephanie felt someone shake her arm.

"Thank God! You've been out for hours, I couldn't wake you," Jan was saying.

She sounded far away. Stephanie opened her eyes and was incredibly relieved to find that she was back in Marlin, in her pyjamas, safe in her own bed at The Lodge. She was home. She sat up quickly.

"You're really you!" she said, with a smile. Jan looked confused, and worried.

"Jan! What day is it?" she demanded.

"Monday. Why?" answered Jan, looking at her closely and putting a hand on Stephanie's forehead to check for a fever. "Steph, you're worrying me. What do you mean I'm real?"

"I meant the date, I need the date," Stephanie said.

"7th February. Why do you need the... where are you going?"

Jan called after her as she ran downstairs to her office to start up her laptop. Stephanie had a nasty headache, her eyes were gritty and sore, and the thought of navigating the internet on the smaller screen of her phone didn't appeal. Jan followed her into the kitchen where she found her filling the kettle.

"I'll do that, let me make you some tea. What's going on, Steph?" she asked, looking concerned.

"What happened yesterday or Friday? I don't know which," Stephanie asked, looking as confused as she felt.

"Nothing unusual. We went out for a pizza last night, had a few glasses of wine then went to bed around midnight. It's two clock, Steph. I've been trying to wake you for hours! You were restless and talking in your sleep, something about a village and a flood? You told me to go at one point! Was it a nightmare?"

Over a welcome cup of tea, Stephanie told Jan about the village and everything else that had happened. She had no choice, Jan wouldn't let her near her laptop till she had.

"It was so real, Jan. Something happened there, I just know it, or is about to…" she said.

"Well it sounds like a vision, or some sort of astral projection, you know, an out-of-body experience. Either way, it seems like there are several spirits that need to be laid to rest, and someone needed your help enough to put you through all that. So, let's see what we can find out!"

Stephanie turned to Jan with tears streaming down her face and gave her a hug.

"I'm so glad you're you," she said, staring at her.

"Me too!" said Jan smiling.

Jan scoured news and historical websites using her phone while Stephanie did the same on her laptop.

"I found some articles about a Welsh valley that was flooded over fifty years ago," said Jan, "but it was cleared of all buildings first and all residents were moved to safety well before the flooding took place."

Stephanie looked at the photographs and shook her head. It looked nothing like Pentre Brân.

"Maybe the flood was symbolic," said Jan, "as your visions often are."

"If that's the case, then this one is beyond vague," said Stephanie. "There are usually some recognisable features for us to go on."

"Maybe there are, and you're just not seeing them yet," suggested Jan.

They both carried on looking. Stephanie tried to put all her preconceptions aside. The village wasn't real, so the chances were that the flood wasn't either. It was all somehow symbolic with a thread of truth, yet that truth was still just beyond her grasp. She focused on what she was sure about: the people. The players in this ghastly story that someone had created to trap her within a fictional village inside her own mind.

Half an hour later, as Stephanie went through

pages and pages of online news stories and images, she finally came across an old photograph in a newspaper article, and her heart skipped a beat.

"It's her!" she said. "Sioned!"

The photograph showed a young blonde woman with a small girl. It was part of an article from - February 1817. Two hundred years ago.

"That fits. She said it was the anniversary today," Stephanie said. "But it's the bicentenary!"

"What happened?" asked Jan.

Stephanie showed her the article. Jan stared at the page before her.

It said that on the night of the 7th of February 1817, a young local woman named Janet Simpson (recently widowed) disappeared with her daughter Flora, aged seven, in mysterious circumstances. They lived at Brook House in Wishill Street, in the village of Crowley, near Welchmoor in Cornwall. It seems that they went for a walk in the middle of a terrible storm and failed to return home. They were never seen alive again, and no bodies were ever found. Her elderly grandmother Elizabeth, and her niece

Sarah (Janet's mother) apparently left the village too soon after, along with Sarah's husband Mansell.

"It's her, I just know it. It all fits!" Stephanie said. "Janet is the English version if Sioned, and Bessie is a nickname for Elizabeth. Brook House is a translation of Tŷ Nant and Wishill is a shortened form of Wish Hill, representing the mountain where the wishing tree stood. The crow in Crowley represents Pentre Brân, Crow Village. And Welch is the old way of spelling Welsh, which is where the Welsh link comes from. Don't you see? We have to go there, Jan. Where is it? Get directions while I dress!"

Jan just nodded in amazement while Stephanie closed the lid of her laptop and ran upstairs. To her further surprise, when she found a map, she saw that Crowley was only fifteen miles away inland from Marlin.

Stephanie fought back the tears as she pulled on her jeans and a jumper. Sioned, or Janet, a woman who went missing two hundred years ago, had sent Stephanie a version of her story in the most intricate of ways because her soul could not rest. She swore to herself that she would not let her down. Sioned's story would be told.

***

Jan drove in silence while Stephanie gathered her thoughts. Soon they arrived at the village of Crowley. It was very similar to the village that Stephanie had seen in her vision, with a few differences.

"This is it," she said.

There were no mountains, just gently rolling hills, and there was also no river. It turned out that the main road through the village was, in fact, Wishill Street. They drove past the cottage by the stream; a sign outside said Brook House. It was the house where they had stayed on her vision. The tearoom from the vision was a bustling café, and the sweet shop was still a sweet shop. The ladieswear shop sold more modern designs than in the illusion, and the camping shop was indeed rammed to the rafters.

"Stop just after the crossroads," said Stephanie.

The pub was there too, named "The Blackheart" and it had the same dragon on the sign. Jan pulled into the car park of the pub

"I think we need to climb to where the wishing tree stood," said Stephanie.

Jan groaned. Although relieved that it meant a hill walk instead of hiking up a mountain, she wasn't fond of walking uphill either.

But as Jan locked the car, Stephanie saw Sioned beckoning to them from the road beyond the crossroads, which had previously been blanketed with fog in her vision of the village. Jan sighed with relief at her lucky escape, and they walked over to greet Sioned.

She was wearing a long grey skirt down to the floor, a white blouse with a frilled high collar, a grey jacket with small grey buttons, and black lace-up shoes. Her hair was worn in a neat bun with wisps that hung either side of her face, and her lovely eyes glistened with tears which fell onto her cheeks. Her skin looked as grey as her clothing.

"I knew you'd come!" she said.

"What really happened here, Sioned, sorry, Janet," Stephanie said.

"It's OK, my grandfather was a Welsh minister," she said. "My family were Welsh, and they used to call me Sioned. You can too."

She turned and walked off down the road and they followed her. There were no houses here, but soon they arrived at an empty, old church.

"This is where my husband had his ministry," said Sioned.

"So, he was a minister too," Stephanie said. Sioned nodded.

She remembered that the article had said that Sioned was a widow. Before she could ask how he died, Sioned said simply, "Influenza." In the days before modern medicine, many thousands of people died of the flu or its complications.

Sioned walked over to a row of graves near the church door.

"Here he is," she said pointing to his grave. Then, "We're not in there," she said mournfully, pointing to headstones bearing her name and that of her daughter. Her husband's grave stood between them.

Stephanie assumed that, at some point, empty coffins had been laid to rest by their family in their memory, as was the custom when no bodies were found.

Sioned carried on walking past an old elm tree and came to a path leading through a black, wrought iron gate. They followed her in silence. Soon the path stared going uphill. Up and up they walked until they came to the top of a tall hill. Jan sighed. At the top, Sioned pointed.

"There," she said coldly. "We're in there."

Stephanie and Jan looked at each other in horror.

They stood at the top of a quarry face, obviously disused for many years, and below them lay a deep, dark pool. Sioned and her daughter had drowned, as she had shown Stephanie. But in a totally different way.

Stephanie and Jan peered cautiously over the edge without getting too close. It was a long way down and the black water looked deep.

"What happened?" asked Stephanie.

Sioned looked out over the quarry, and her voice was almost a whisper.

"My family wanted to leave the village, you see. My husband was supporting them, but when he died, we had very little income. Bessie persuaded the others to leave. It was all her fault. She wanted to go back to Wales. I didn't want to go, I couldn't leave my James all alone in that graveyard. So, I brought Flora up here, took her in my arms and jumped."

Her voice was flat and emotionless. Stephanie and Jan stared at her in disbelief and disgust. Sioned had killed herself and her little girl. As in the vision, in Sioned's mind she blamed Bessie for everything. She could see the truth now. It was nothing to do with Bessie at all; Sioned had orchestrated everything. She had forced the old woman to threaten them, or even imitated her as she had done with Jan. Poor Bessie was just another tragic victim of her manipulation, like Sarah and little Flora.

Sioned continued with her awful tale.

"They came looking for me, and I met them up here. I couldn't let them leave, could I?" she continued with a small smile. "Family should stay together! They thought I was still alive, so when I stood close to the edge they tried to grab for me, and they went over. One after another. They can't leave me now!"

Stephanie and Jan were horrified. Maybe she was lost in grief for her dead husband and felt abandoned by him, and fearing that her family would leave without her, her mind had fractured. Or maybe she was just plain evil. Either way, Bessie, Sarah and her grandfather hadn't left the village following her disappearance. Sioned had lured them here and killed them too. Her whole family.

"And now it's your turn!" she said. "You left me too, but you won't leave ever again. Not you or your friend!"

Sioned had turned against Stephanie because she managed to get away, feeling that Stephanie too had rejected her, and Jan was in danger too because she was with her.

Sioned turned towards them smiling and lunged for Stephanie, her eyes wild and dark. Her face was ghoulish in its appearance, as you would expect from a century old skull with its skin stretched tight over bare bone where the flesh had withered beneath. Her clothes were in rags and her skeletal hand reached out to grasp Stephanie by the arm. Stephanie instinctively stepped back, and that step brought her nearer to the edge. Sioned lunged again, grinning in satisfaction.

But Jan was ready for her. To Stephanie's amazement she started reciting an ancient spell, an incantation to put troubled spirits to rest. Sioned stared incredulously at her, unable to move with her hideous death mask frozen in fear. She screamed.

"Please!" she said, stepping back, her face resuming a human appearance. "I'm sorry!"

"No, you're not!" shouted Jan.

As she uttered the final line of the spell, Sioned dissolved into a pile of bones which disintegrated into fragments, and blew away on the breeze like grey snowflakes.

"How did you know...?" Stephanie began, moving away from the precipice.

"While you were dressing, I found this," Jan said.

She took her phone out of her jacket pocket and showed her what she had found.

Stephanie was stunned when she read that there was a local legend about a ghostly figure who would try to lure passers-by to their deaths at the old quarry. The Grey Lady was thought to be responsible for a string of disappearances in the 1800s, but for some reason the sightings had stopped. Until now.

"Ran out of people to trick, I expect," said Jan in her inimitable dry way.

"She didn't want me to tell her story after all, she wanted me to join the others!" said Stephanie in disgust. "But why me?"

"Because she sensed that you could help them escape the village, just like you did," said Jan.

Sioned had concocted the complex vision to trap Stephanie, simply because she sensed that she could release the others. Stephanie realised that the poor souls that she had seen in the village were all people that she had killed. Trapped for eternity at her bidding, maybe in a dreamscape built from their own memories, or maybe dragged from one scenario to another at her will. Imprisoned, just like she would have been, had she not escaped. She felt cold. An icy breeze was rising from the quarry, like an invisible mist.

"In that case, I'm surprised this place isn't

riddled with spirits!" she added.

"Speaking of which..." said Jan, pointing over Stephanie's shoulder.

She turned to see a group of people, all faces she recognised from her vision of Pentre Brân. They had all risen from their resting place, in the cold, deep water at the bottom of the quarry. With Sioned gone, they were free. In the end, by saving Stephanie, Jan had saved them too.

Bessie was there with Sarah, and the man from their bedroom in the vision had his arm round her shoulder: He must have been Mansell, Sarah's husband and Sioned's father. The village shopkeepers, tea room waitress and pub landlord were there too. There were others too, the ones who must have been hiding in the village behind their curtains and blinds, afraid to look outside. Each one was a victim, lured to their death by Sioned. Each one who had told Stephanie that they were sorry had done so because they knew what her fate would be. Jan was right; Sioned wasn't sorry at all.

Then from behind Sioned's father came a little girl, a beautiful child with blonde ringlets and the biggest blue eyes. She wore a long blue dress, black lace-up boots, a white pinafore. The man ushered her forward.

"My name is Flora. It means flowers," she said in a small voice. "Thank you for helping us! I knew you would..."

She took a posy of forget-me-nots which she had been holding behind her back, ran over and threw it into the quarry, as if in remembrance of all the people who had died there. Then she ran to stand beside Bessie.

Stephanie felt an icy chill run down her back. It was Flora who had left the flowers on her bed. Flora who had silently watched her from the window of the pub and sent her clues that what she was experiencing was just a fabrication from the disturbed mind of her desperate mother. Flora's appearance was that of a child, but her soul was that of an old woman, and a clever one. One who had waited a long time to escape from her prison in Pentre Brân, just like the others.

Now Stephanie could help her; she would them all to find the peace they had been denied, some for two hundred years. Stephanie called on Lucas to help them, and a beam of sunlight appeared through a gap in the clouds. That was their way home. She sent out her love to them all, with a silent message that it was time to go. One by one, the people waved and smiled as they walked into the beam of sunlight and vanished, free at last from the clutches of The Grey Lady.

Gone too was Pentre Brân; it had only existed in Stephanie's memory. Or maybe Sioned was destined to wander there alone for eternity, trapped in her own personal version of hell that resembled Crowley, the place that she had never wanted to leave. Stephanie shuddered at the very thought that such things might be possible. Two days had been enough for her.

***

When they arrived back at The Lodge, Jan rang a contact in the local police at Wadebridge and informed them that she had received a tip-off that the quarry was full of bodies and should be drained. The families of Sioned's missing victims needed closure.

Then she went to find Stephanie. She found her standing by the open door in her kitchen, clutching a mug of hot tea while she watched the waves break on the beach below. Gulls cried, buffeted by the same breeze that caused the fluffy clouds to speed across the sky. Children ran and laughed with kites and footballs, and an elderly couple walked their equally elderly golden retriever. Children and animals, things that had been missing from her vison. She should have known then that it couldn't be real.

It was cold with the door open, but she seemed oblivious to it. Stephanie had been shaken by her experience, there was no doubt about that.

"Are you OK?" asked Jan, putting an arm round her shoulder. "Come inside, it's freezing."

Stephanie seemed to register Jan's words although still deep in thought. She stepped inside and closed the door. She turned to face her.

"I never dreamed that spirits could get into your head like that and create their own world. I'm used to getting snippets of memories, warnings and messages. But this… this scares me Jan."

"There's still a lot that we don't know or understand, Steph. This spirit was strong, very strong. To appear so alive, so human that she would lure people to their deaths, and create a whole village to imprison their souls so that they couldn't leave her, well, that takes a lot of power.

Believe me, there is still so much to learn, for both of us. And we will, because we want to help people like Bessie and Sarah. And little Flora."

Stephanie turned to Jan, brushing away a tear. "Yes," she said, "yes, we will!"

"Anyway, you should have known that the whole trip was dodgy when I turned my phone off. You know I wouldn't be able to last ten minutes without it, let alone a whole weekend. And don't even get me started on the mountain walk….!"

Jan continued for some time while Stephanie looked at her smiling.

"Thank you for saving me, at the quarry…" she said.

"That's what friends are for! Got any chocolate biscuits?" said Jan.

Maisy curled around Stephanie's legs waiting to be fed. Stephanie dried her eyes with her sleeve, then she scooped the purring cat up into her arms and hugged her, before putting her back on the floor, handing Jan a packed of chocolate digestives and opening a tin of cat food. She remembered to thank Lucas her guide too, for his help during her nightmarish trip into the dark recesses of Sioned's mind, and she did so silently.

"It's good to be home!" she thought.

Then an invisible presence spoke right next to her.

"ENJOY IT WHILE YOU CAN," warned Lucas.

THE END

ACKNOWLEDGEMENTS

My thanks, as always, to my family and friends: for their support, advice and suggestions, and also to my daughter for her invaluable editorial input and cover art, and to my husband for the cover photograph. Also thank you to you, for reading this novella.

As those that have read the first novel in my series The Marlin Chronicles will know, this is a stand-alone story which can be enjoyed at any time along your journey through the series. It takes place between books 1 and 2 and I was careful not to give away spoilers. But it includes a few hints about Stephanie and her best friend Jan which readers of Book 1: Mother of Marlin will recognise, and I think it leads neatly into Book 2: Children of Marlin, which is due for publication soon.

Those who have read the brief bio on my Amazon author page, or the extended version on my website, will already know that I am Welsh. I am proud of that fact, and I have a degree in Welsh to prove it. The idea behind this novella was for me to write about somewhere else close to my heart; somewhere that my family and friends can relate to. As always, they are my inspiration, as are those that are no longer with me, and I couldn't have written this story without any of them.

Wales truly is a beautiful land of music, magic and mystery, and if you have never had the pleasure to visit, I strongly recommend it. Yet again, I have included in this story several snippets of folklore and historical references, and a large helping of the paranormal. I hope you enjoyed it, wherever you live, and wherever your roots lie, and as this story shows, they might not be the same place. Home is where you want it to be.

FEEDBACK AND FREEBIES

As usual, your comments and feedback are so important to me. I welcome your reviews on Amazon and Goodreads, and I give my thanks to those that have already taken the time to write a review. But as always, please don't give away any spoilers! You can contact me on Facebook too, or via my website.

I would love to add you to my new e-mail list. You will have access to any website members' page; it contains all new information about The Marlin Chronicles series which is posted there before it is made available elsewhere (such as sequel descriptions, cover art, release dates, compilations and other bonus content.) To sign up, just go to my website and use the form provided or contact me via Facebook or email. All I need is your email address (name optional, but it would be better to know who I'm emailing). Email list bonuses might include book previews, book cover releases, sequel descriptions, even free early access to another novella like this one (which was a free gift to my list members, pre-publication on Amazon).

I will not pass your email/name on to any third party, or send you any other information apart from that which relates to The Marlin Chronicles series.

Website: alysonmountjoyauthor.yolasite.com

Facebook: facebook.com/alysonmountjoyauthor/

Email: alyson.mountjoy.ebooks@aol.co.uk

ALREADY AVAILABLE ON AMAZON:

The Marlin Chronicles Series, Book 1: Mother of Marlin:
https://www.amazon.co.uk/dp/B06XJD1TVK/ref=sr_1_1?ie=UTF8&qid=1489253703&sr=8-1&keywords=mother+of+marlin

COMING SOON ON AMAZON:

The sequels currently written and awaiting publication are:

Book 2: "Children of Marlin."

Book 3: "Whispers of Marlin."

Book 4: "Nightmares of Marlin."

Marlin has many more secrets to tell; I hope you will join me there.

Alyson Mountjoy – May 2017.

Printed in Great Britain
by Amazon